THIS
BOOK
BELONGS TO

_____

Guy Gilchrist's TINY DINOS

SIR WALDO'S ISLAND ADVENTURE

AS TOLD BY COREY NASH

BASED ON AN ORIGINAL
STORY BY GUY AND BRAD GILCHRIST

WARNER
JUVENILE
BOOKS
A Warner Communications Company
NEW YORK

FOR LAUREN AND
GARRETT, WHO LOVED THE
DINOS FIRST.
LOVE,
DADDY

For Mom and Dad, who started my writing career with a
toy typewriter and lots of books!
—C.N.

Warner Juvenile Books Edition
Copyright © 1988 by United Feature Syndicate, Inc.
All rights reserved.

Warner Books, Inc., 666 Fifth Avenue, New York, NY 10103
Ⓦ A Warner Communications Company

Printed in the United States of America
First Warner Juvenile Books Printing: March 1988
10 9 8 7 6 5 4 3 2 1

Library of Congress Cataloging in Publication Data

Gilchrist, Guy.
  Guy Gilchrist's Tiny Dinos Sir Waldo's island
adventure.

  Summary: The story of how Sir Waldo Rhumba discovered the
Tiny Dinos.
  [1. Dinosaurs—Fiction.   2. Children's stories]
I. Nash, Corey. II. Gilchrist, Brad. III. Title.
IV. Title: Tiny dinos Sir Waldo's island adventure.
PZ8.3.G39Gw 1988   [E]   87-40332
ISBN 1-55782-010-4

SIR WALDO'S ISLAND ADVENTURE

Meet Sir Waldo Rhumba, world's greatest explorer and adventurer. World-shaking discoveries happen daily to Sir Waldo, who roams the seven seas in his flying submarine, *The Jolly Turtle*. It can soar above the clouds, it can skim

the water's surface at record-breaking speeds, and it can travel deep down to the ocean's floor.

We all know that Sir Waldo discovered the Hanging Gardens of Dandelion. The whole world heard about when he unearthed King Putt-Putt's tomb. But Sir Waldo's greatest discovery has been kept a secret. Until now...

It all began three months ago. Sir Waldo was zooming along in *The Jolly Turtle*, and he was just starting to get a little bit impatient. After all, it had been at least ten minutes since his last discovery!

"Humpf! Nothing in sight," the great explorer said. "Hello? Am I talking to myself?! Yoo-hoo, Tort! Having a little nap, are we?"

At that, his ever faithful companion, Tort, popped his head

out. Tort is a box turtle who lives in one of Sir Waldo's many pockets. Tort doesn't talk, but he "speaks" to Sir Waldo by using his own special sign language.

"Let's go down!" Tort pointed.

"That's exactly what I was doing," Sir Waldo answered.

The Jolly Turtle cruised along the ocean's sandy bottom, surrounded by all sorts of strange sea life.

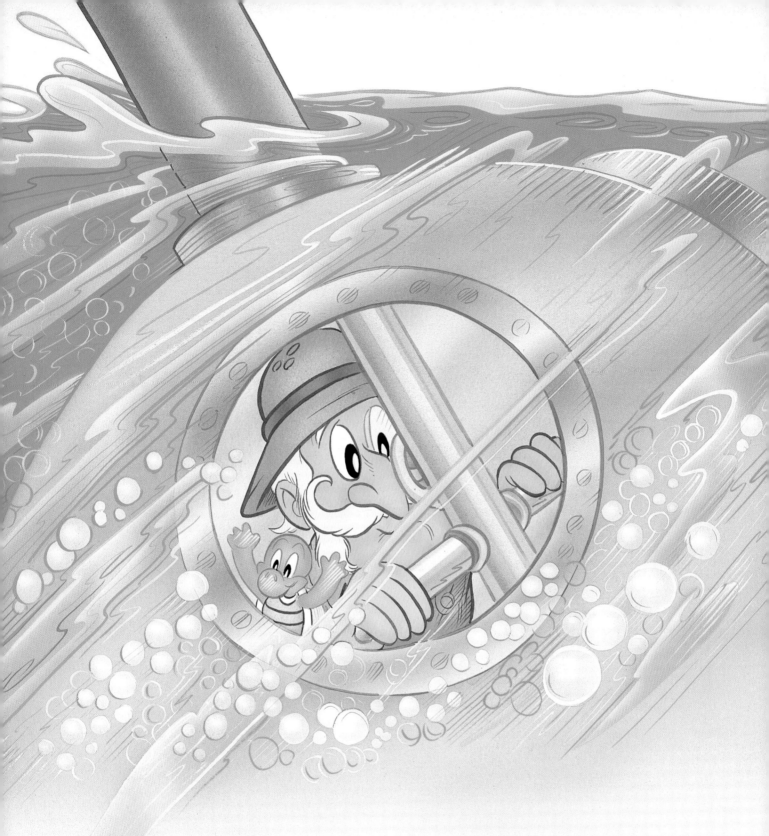

They had traveled several miles when Tort suddenly
motioned, "Time to go up!"

"Well, of *course*, Tort. That's just what I was about to do
when you interrupted me again," Sir Waldo replied.

When they reached the surface,
they saw a tropical island in

the distance. Several volcanoes loomed large on the horizon,
and palm trees stood out against the clear blue sky.

"Aha! This is obviously an uncharted island, completely unknown to *anyone*. And I, the great Sir Waldo Rhumba, have discovered it! I name thee Rhumba Island!"

A great sense of adventure came over Sir Waldo as he and Tort started ashore.

It was soon clear to the explorer that no people lived on this island. But that doesn't mean *no one* lived there. Monkeys, lions, jungle cats, crocodiles, snakes, and tropical birds scurried everywhere, not to mention some weird wildlife that only

someone with Sir Waldo's vast knowledge could identify.

Colorful plants and all kinds of luscious fruits completed the scene. It was heaven on earth.

Well, almost. Sir Waldo was so involved in exploring this strange new land that he did not notice a mischievous monkey aiming a coconut directly at the adventurer's helmet. Before Tort could warn him, Sir Waldo got bonked on the head and fell backward, right into an underground cavern!

Once Sir Waldo's head cleared, he and Tort wound through the dark, mysterious cave.

"Ho, ho, Tort! I have discovered an underground cavern! Let us explore its depths."

And so the two made their way through the twists and turns of the cave, only to reach a dead end.

"Of course! An empty cavern! Exactly as I suspected. Let's return to *The Jolly Turtle* and—"

But as he spoke, something light reflected off his flashlight's beam.

"Aha! Just as I thought! Six giant eggs!" Sir Waldo tried to lift one, but it was much too heavy.

"Tort, I realize that an amateur such as you would have no idea how to get the eggs out of this cave and into the warm sunlight where they will hatch. But I, on the other hand, am

prepared to construct a pulley and bring the eggs outside so that *you* may find out what's inside my newest discovery."

One by one, the explorer carefully rolled each egg to the cave's opening and hoisted it up.

It took a while, but finally Sir Waldo moved the six mysterious eggs into the sun.

Bursting with excitement, he eagerly waited for the eggs to hatch.

And waited...

And waited...

"These eggs are never going to hatch!"
Sir Waldo said. "Let's move on."

As the explorer and Tort made their way back to *The Jolly Turtle*, they suddenly heard a loud rumbling noise.

Then the ground under their feet began to vibrate! Rocks came tumbling down on them!

"Take cover, Tort! This is obviously a volcano about to erupt!"

Tort, being closer to the ground, knew it was the eggs.

RUMBLE!

RUMBLE!

Sure enough, the eggs were shuddering and starting to crack. Before Sir Waldo could get his camera ready,

the largest egg was cracking open. Slowly, slowly, at first, then
pop! Sir Waldo stood face-to-face with the most incredible
creature he had ever seen in his life!

"*A baby brontosaurus!* Of course. I knew it all along! These
are six brontosaurus eggs. Naturally, Tort, you must know
that the brontosaurus was one of the largest dinosaurs ever to
walk the earth."

While Sir Waldo was rattling off his knowledge, the eggs continued to hatch. One! Two! Three! Four! Four more baby dinosaurs!

"Great prehistory, Tort!" Sir Waldo identified each dinosaur as it hatched—a baby triceratops, a baby pteranodon, a baby stegosaurus, and a baby plateosaurus.

"Tort, you have witnessed the greatest discovery known to civilization! I, Sir Waldo Rhumba, have found dinosaurs—*alive in the twentieth century!* I shall call them 'Tiny Dinos.'"

There was one egg left. Sir Waldo approached it. And with a great roar, a baby tyrannosaurus rex emerged.

This baby was born to be hungry and didn't waste any time in eating his eggshell.

"Ha, ha!" Tort laughed. "Boy, was that Tiny Dino angry! He thought you were going to eat his shell first!"

But Sir Waldo was otherwise engaged....

The explorer came to in the arms of the baby brontosaurus, being hugged and kissed. Sir Waldo curiously watched as the Tiny Dinos started playing and goofing around.

The baby plateosaurus was the only Tiny Dino who could walk—and the first one to play!

"He's not chasing you, silly," Tort said to the shy stegosaurus. "He's only being playful!"

The spunky pteranodon spread her wings and tried to fly.
But she wound up spending most of her time on the ground,
which was trembling from the fierce roar of the baby
tyrannosaurus rex—or was it his stomach?

GLOMP

Tort motioned to Sir Waldo, "Better feed these babies fast!"

The explorer quickly gathered food for them. *Of course* he knew exactly what dinosaurs liked to eat.

"Lunch is served, Tiny Dinos! Let's see," Sir Waldo said to the pteranodon. "Because you are the smallest, I shall call you Tiny Ptery. Naturally, you'll love this fish.

"And I have a special treat for you plant-eaters. For you, my Triceratot, some lovely ferns. Cactus for our Baby Steggie, but watch out for the needles! Playful Plateo, you rascal! You went straight for the bananas!

"Well, just help yourselves, Baby Bronty and Baby Rex!" Sir Waldo said to the two as they dug in. Rex took Sir Waldo's lunch and ate it, brown bag and all!

"Rex, that bag will give you an upset stomach!"

"A *tin can* wouldn't bother that baby's belly!" Tort thought to himself.

Now that the Dinos had been fed, Sir Waldo returned to *The Jolly Turtle* to take care of the rest of their needs.

"Tort, I've never raised a baby before, much less six baby dinosaurs, but of course *I* know precisely what they need. Oh, they are fortunate that Sir Waldo Rhumba discovered them instead of someone else. But then, who else *but* the great Sir Waldo could have made a discovery such as this!"

Sir Waldo muttered to himself as he quickly assembled the gear. "First, they'll need bonnets to protect their precious heads from the tropical sun. Diapers, of course. Bottles! Rattles!"

The explorer even made some special surprises for the Dinos. Ptery got a scarf and some airplane goggles. "Bronty, you are much more comfortable in water than on land because you are so big," Sir Waldo said as he waded out to give her an extra large bonnet and sunglasses.

"Shy Steggie, here's your very own security blanket. And Tot, look what I've made for you!" the adventurer said as Triceratot admired herself in her mica mirror.

Plateo got just what he wanted—a baseball bat, a coconut ball, and a silly baseball cap. But the happiest Tiny Dino of all was Rex!

"Whew," thought Tort. "Now that he's got all of that food, he won't think of eating *me*!"

As time passed, Sir Waldo taught the Tiny Dinos how to take care of themselves on Rhumba Island. They learned to walk and talk, but most of all, they liked to play. Especially Plateo!

Ptery became an ace flyer, and Tot spent lots of time lazing around on the beach watching her. Rex never ran out of things to do!

And always, Bronty was there to watch over the other Dinos, particularly Steggie, who needed lots of hugs and affection.

After lunch each day, the Dinos
went to school, where Sir Waldo
taught them to read and write,
and many other things.

"Look, Uncle Waldo! What's that?"
Ptery asked during a spelling lesson.

"Why, that's an iguana. Did you know that he's a relative of yours? Iguanas are tiny, modern-day versions of the prehistoric dinosaurs."

"Does that mean I can't eat him?" Rex asked.

"Class dismissed," Sir Waldo sighed.

"Coconut ball!" Plateo shouted.

EAT FOOD

While the Dinos played coconut ball, Sir Waldo went back to *The Jolly Turtle*. Just as he finished writing his two hundredth book, a message came over the transmitter.

"Calling Sir Waldo Rhumba! The Explorers Club of the World has named you Explorer of the Century. Your award will be presented tomorrow at noon at Club Headquarters. Do you read me?"

"I shall be delighted to attend! Roger wilko and out!"

To Tort he said, "Well, it certainly took them *long enough*! I can't *wait* until they see the Tiny Dinos! Then they will surely rename the award Greatest Explorer of All Time!" Sir Waldo was very satisfied with himself, but deep down something was bothering him.

"Alas, Tort, I cannot bring the Dinos to civilization. At least not yet. Although they are old enough to take care of themselves, they are still too young to face the world. No, you and I shall leave in the morning while they are still asleep. They will be fine here on their own. Bronty will take care of them."

Before the sun came up the next day, *The Jolly Turtle* was revved up and ready to go. But it never left the lagoon.

"I cannot do it, Tort! No, I simply cannot leave the Tiny Dinos, now or ever! No award in the world could give me the joy that they bring. We're staying, but the award *must* remain a secret between us."

Neither of them saw an impish monkey listening nearby. This monkey had a big mouth and couldn't wait to wake up the Dinos and tell them.

the Jolly Turtle

"Gosh," Bronty said, "Uncle Waldo's been *so* good to us, and now he's giving up the biggest honor of his life just to stay here with *us*!"

"I know!" Tot piped up. "Let's give him our *own* award!"

"But it's *got* to be a surprise," Ptery added.

"A surprise party!" shouted Plateo.

"Yeah, with plenty of food!" (That was Rex's idea.)

The monkey promised that he and his friends would keep Sir Waldo busy while the Dinos got the party going. The gang was silly and very excited as they ran around making decorations and gathering party food.

At last, everything was ready.

"Uncle Waldo, can you come here and help me, please?" Steggie cried out.

"SURPRISE, UNCLE WALDO!!"

DINO UNCLE OF THE CENTURY

THANK YOU FOR BRINGING US OUT OF OUR SHELLS

Sir Waldo was so touched that he forgot himself for a second.

"A shell-a-bration! I'm egg-static! This is the best award in the entire universe!"

"Uncle Waldo, you're dino-mite! We love you!" Bronty said.
"And I love you all too."
"Okay, okay, enough of this mushy stuff. Let's eat!" said Rex.